New Mexico

for Kids

A Travel Guide for Young People
Written and illustrated by Lynnell Diamond

PUBLISHED BY OTTER BE READING BOOKS
PO Box 10130
Chicago, IL 60610

New Mexico is called the Land of Enchantment

The flag of New Mexico is bright yellow with an orange sun in the middle. This sun symbol was first used by the Zia people. It stands for friendship and peace. The Zia are Native Americans who have lived in the place we call New Mexico for hundreds of years. You'll see the Zia sun symbol on New Mexico license plates, too.

The state flower is the yucca. Read some interesting things about it on page 43.

The state animal is the black bear. You can see one on page 39.

The state tree is the pinyon (pin-YONE). Read about them on page 43.

coelophysis

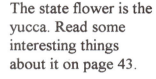

AM I BEAUTIFUL, OR WHAT?

yucca

New Mexico has a state fossil. Its name is coelophysis (see-lo-FY-sis). Read more about it on page 7.

New Mexico's state bird is the roadrunner. It is sometimes called paisano (pie-SAH-no), a Spanish word that means "fellow traveler" or "friend." It's also called "the clown of the desert."

Native Americans have legends about the courage and cleverness of the roadrunner. Roadrunners move quickly across the desert, searching for insects and lizards to eat. They also eat cactus fruit, scorpions, tarantulas, and even rattlesnakes. Roadrunners have four toes, two that point forward and two that point back. This makes them leave unusual X-shaped tracks in the sand.

There are 19 roadrunners in this book. Can you find them all? Count the cover, but not the answer page.

It's a land of enchanting places...

This is Shiprock, the plug (center part) of an old volcano. It rises 1,700 feet above the plains around it. That's more than five football fields stacked end to end! Shiprock is on the Navajo reservation in northwestern New Mexico. The Navajo people call it *Tse Bida Hi*, which means "rock with wings." They believe the mountain was once a giant bird that carried their ancestors on its back to this land.

Can you find it?

In the center of this book you'll find a pull-out map of New Mexico. Can you find Shiprock on the map? The coordinates for Shiprock are 1-A. When you find it, put a check mark in this box.

I found Shiprock on the map!

3

...and enchanting people.

In New Mexico, about one person in every ten is a Native American. Most are Pueblo, Navajo, or Apache.

About four in every ten people in New Mexico are Hispanic. They are people whose ancestors came from Mexico or Spain.

Everyone else in New Mexico is called Anglo. These are people whose ancestors came from Europe, Africa, China, Japan, the Middle East, or anywhere else on earth!

Some of New Mexico's people are famous!

Use the code at the bottom of the page to fill in the blanks below.
The words will tell you what these people are famous for.

Tony Hillerman and John Nichols are

W R I T E R S
23 18 9 20 5 18 19

Tony Hillerman writes mystery stories about New Mexico's Navajo people.
John Nichols wrote *The Milagro Beanfield War*, which was made into a movie.

Al Unser Sr., Al Unser Jr., and Bobby Unser are ___ ___ ___ ___ ___ ___ ___
18 1 3 5 3 1 18

___ ___ ___ ___ ___ ___ ___ . They have all competed in the Indy 500.
4 18 9 22 5 18 19

Maxie Anderson and Ben Abruzzo were the first people to fly a ___ ___ ___ ___ ___ ___
8 15 20 1 9 18

___ ___ ___ ___ ___ ___ ___ across the Atlantic ocean.
2 1 12 12 15 15 14

Nancy Lopez is a championship ___ ___ ___ ___ ___ ___ .
7 15 12 6 5 18

Michael Martin Murphy is a country-western ___ ___ ___ ___ ___ ___ .
He recorded a song called "Wildfire."   19 9 14 7 5 18

Trent Dimas and Lance Ringnald are Olympic ___ ___ ___ ___ ___ ___ ___ ___ .
Trent Dimas won a gold medal in 1992.   7 25 13 14 1 19 20 19

Georgia O'Keeffe and R. C. Gorman are ___ ___ ___ ___ ___ ___ ___ . You will see their
paintings in art galleries in New Mexico. 1 18 20 9 19 20 19

Harrison Schmidt, Mike Mulane, and Sid Gutierrez are ___ ___ ___ ___ ___ ___ ___ ___ ___ ___
1 19 20 18 15 14 1 21 20 19

Shane Andrews, Steve Ontiveros, and Ralph Kiner are ___ ___ ___ ___ ___ ___ ___ ___ players.
2 1 19 5 2 1 12 12

William Hanna and Bill Watterson are ___ ___ ___ ___ ___ ___ ___ ___ ___ ___ ___
3 1 18 20 15 15 14 9 19 20 19

Bill Watterson draws "Calvin and Hobbes." William Hanna created Yogi Bear, the Flintstones, and the Jetsons.

Clyde Tombaugh is the astronomer who discovered ___ ___ ___ ___ ___ .
16 12 21 20 15

1	2	3	4	5	6	7	8	9	10	11	12	13	14	15	16	17	18	19	20	21	22	23	24	25	26
A	B	C	D	E	F	G	H	I	J	K	L	M	N	O	P	Q	R	S	T	U	V	W	X	Y	Z

A long, long time ago...

The place we call New Mexico has been here for a VERY long time - more than a billion years. During that long time, the land changed many times. Sometimes it was a swamp. Sometimes it was covered with water. Often, volcanoes erupted and left behind large lava flows. You can still see these lava flows in New Mexico.

I found Capulin Volcano on the map! (6-A)

Capulin Volcano last erupted about 10,000 years ago

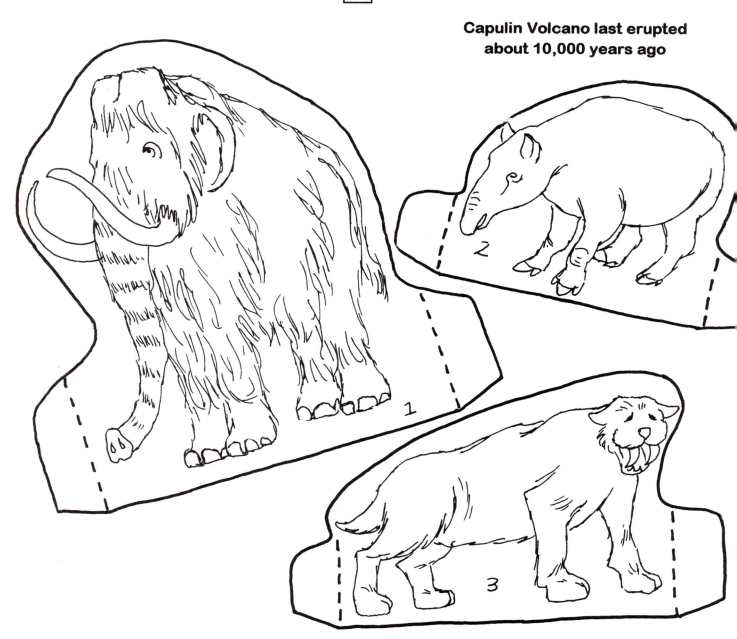

Many kinds of creatures once lived in New Mexico that don't live here - or anywhere - any more. These pictures are of some of the animals that lived here at different times in the ancient past. Do you know the names of these animals? Read each paragraph at the top of the next page. Then find the animal you think the paragraph is about. Put the number that's by the animal in the space by the paragraph that describes it.

You can make stand-ups with these animals. Color them and cut them out. Then glue them to thin cardboard, like an empty cereal box. Cut them out again, and fold back at the dotted lines.

_____4_____ *Allosaurus* grew to about forty feet. Its jagged teeth and sharp claws made it a fierce fighter.

_____3_____ The *saber-toothed tiger* had enormous teeth, and might have used them on early humans!

_____1_____ The *wooly mammoth* looked like a shaggy elephant with curly tusks.

_____5_____ *Coelophysis* (the New Mexico state dinosaur) was small and very fast. It was about 6 feet long and weighed about 50 pounds. How much do you weigh?

_____2_____ The *tapir* had a long, strange-looking nose that it used to pick up its food.

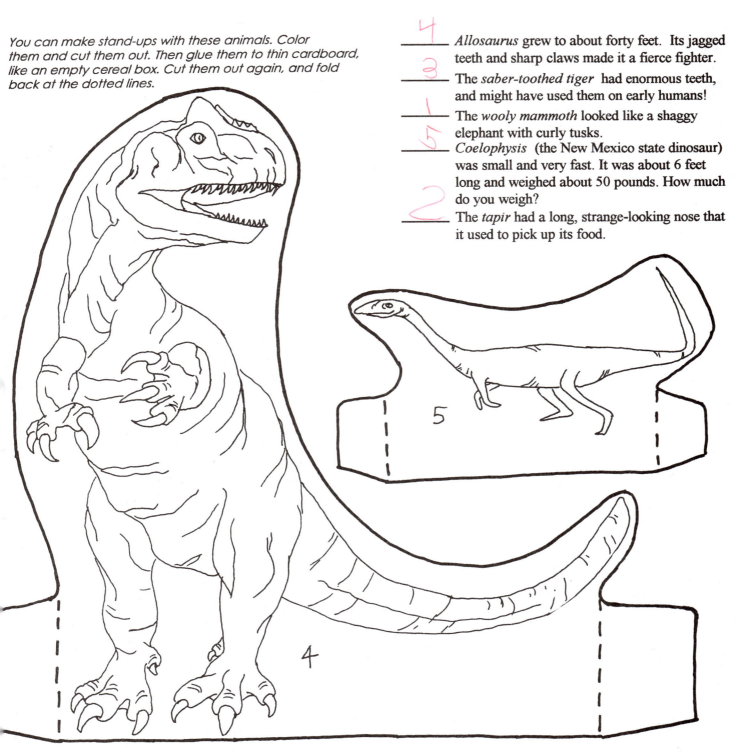

Learn more about dinosaurs at...

Clayton Dinosaur Trackway at Clayton Lake State Park near the town of Clayton. At least eight kinds of dinosaurs lived here at one time. You can still see their tracks.

New Mexico Museum of Natural History, in Albuquerque's Old Town. This is a great place to go. It has dinosaur bones and stories, an active volcano model, a time machine, and a Dynamax Theater.

The Florence Hawley Ellis Museum of Anthropology at Ghost Ranch near Abiquiu. Coelophysis once lived around here, and left some bones behind.

You can see lava fields at...

Valley of Fires State Park, west of Carrizozo. The rock here is very sharp - stay on the trails and always wear shoes. This lava is from a volcano that erupted about 2000 years ago.

Capulin Mountain National Monument, near Raton. This volcano is 10,000 years old. You can hike around the rim or into the crater. Capulin may erupt again some day.

El Malpais National Conservation Area near Grants. You'll see lots of lava and strange rock formations.

New Mexico's first people

Humans have been living in New Mexico for more than 35,000 years. We know they were here because they left behind the tools and weapons they used to hunt the mammoths, camels, huge buffalo, and other creatures that also lived here then. About 5,000 years ago, the people began to carve and paint pictures on the rocks around them. We can still see some of these pictures in New Mexico. Pictures that were painted are called pictographs. If they were carved or pecked into the rock, we call them petroglyphs.

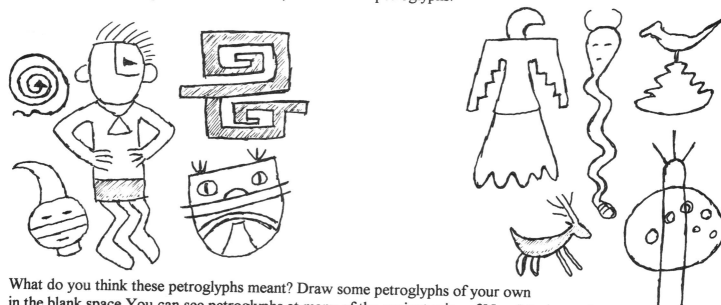

What do you think these petroglyphs meant? Draw some petroglyphs of your own in the blank space. You can see petroglyphs at many of the ancient ruins of New Mexico and at:

Three Rivers Petroglyph National Recreation Site, north of Tularosa. There are more than 500 petroglyphs along a one-mile trail.

Petroglyph National Monument, west of Albuquerque. Four walking tours go past more than 10,000 rock drawings. **Remember, you should NEVER touch petroglyphs anywhere in New Mexico, or carve or mark on rocks.**

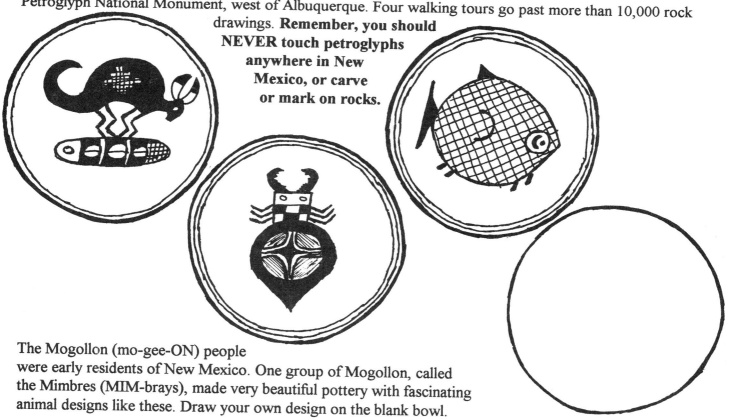

The Mogollon (mo-gee-ON) people were early residents of New Mexico. One group of Mogollon, called the Mimbres (MIM-brays), made very beautiful pottery with fascinating animal designs like these. Draw your own design on the blank bowl.

Anasazi, the Amazing "Ancient Ones"

For over 1,500 years, a fascinating group of native people lived in New Mexico. They are called Anasazi, which means "the ancient ones." The Anasazi built houses of rock and mud, often in cliffs where they were sheltered from weather and enemies. Some of the houses, called pueblos (PWEB-loze), had hundreds of rooms and were home to thousands of people.

The Anasazi grew corn, beans, squash, and melons. They learned to use water in ditches to irrigate their crops. They made clay pots and wove beautiful baskets to store the food in. They built hundreds of roads across the mountains and plains so that they could trade with their neighbors.

The Anasazi mysteriously abandoned their homes about 700 years ago. But we can still see the remains of many of the pueblos today. Below is a maze of a pueblo ruin at Chaco Culture National Historical Park, which is south of Farmington. Can you find your way from start to finish?

I found Chaco Canyon on the map! (2-B) ☐

See Anasazi ruins and learn more about these amazing people at...

Aztec Ruins National Monument, near the town of Aztec; Bandelier National Monument, near Los Alamos; Gila Cliff Dwellings National Monument, north of Silver City; Puye Cliff Dwellings on the Santa Clara Pueblo south of Espanola; Salmon Ruin and Heritage Park, near Farmington. During the summer, you can see a musical play about the Anasazi called "Anasazi, the Ancient Ones," at Lions Wilderness Park near Farmington.

El Morro, New Mexico's "Autograph Rock"

About 450 years ago, Spanish explorers came to New Mexico. They were looking for cities made of gold that the natives of Mexico had told them about. They called these cities of gold the Seven Cities of Cibola. One of the first explorers was Francisco Vasquez de Coronado. He conquered many of the native villages in New Mexico and gave the area its name. In Spanish, the name is Nuevo Mejico (new-AY-vo MAY-hee-ko). But Coronado never found the cities of gold.

When Spanish settlers were ready to move into New Mexico, they built a road north from Mexico. They called it El Camino Real (el cuh-Mee-no ray-ALL), which means Royal Road. Today, an interstate highway follows the same path to Santa Fe.

There is a mountain in western New Mexico called El Morro, or Inscription Rock. At the bottom of the mountain, the name Juan de Onate is carved into the rock. Onate was a Spanish explorer who carved his name there in 1605. Other explorers and settlers left their names on the rock, and native people left petroglyphs. You can still see them today.

See if you can find Onate's name in the drawing of El Morro below. (You can write your name on this drawing, but NOT on the real rock!)

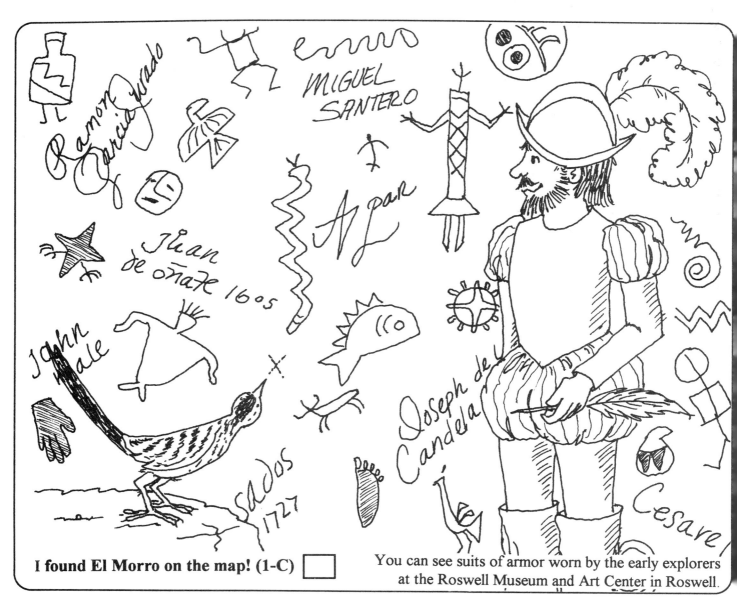

I found El Morro on the map! (1-C) ☐

You can see suits of armor worn by the early explorers at the Roswell Museum and Art Center in Roswell.

The Pueblo Revolt and Old Man Gloom

The Spanish explorers and settlers were not always kind to the native people of New Mexico. Most of the native people lived in pueblos, like their ancestors, the Anasazi. They were peaceful farmers. They were also deeply religious. But the Spanish forced them to give up their religion. Sometimes they treated the Pueblo people like slaves.

In 1598, the people of Acoma Pueblo rebelled against the Spanish. Acoma is called "Sky City," because it is on top of a high mesa (MAY-suh), a flat-topped mountain with steep sides. It was very hard to scale these cliffs. But after several months the Spanish were finally able to reach the top, and they killed hundreds of the Pueblo people.

Almost a hundred years later, a Pueblo leader named Pope (po-PAY) led another revolt. The native people killed 400 of the Spanish settlers. The settlers who survived moved back to Mexico. But in 1692, a Spanish leader named Diego de Vargas (dee-AY-go day VAR-gus) lead the Spanish settlers back into New Mexico and conquered the Pueblo people once again. Every year in Santa Fe, there is a big celebration called a fiesta (fee-ES-tah) to remember the day when the Spanish came back to New Mexico. During the fiesta, a big, ugly man made of paper is burned in a bonfire. His name is Zozobra, or Old Man Gloom. When Zozobra is gone, everyone is happy!

Connect the dots from 1 to 58 to see a picture of Zozobra.

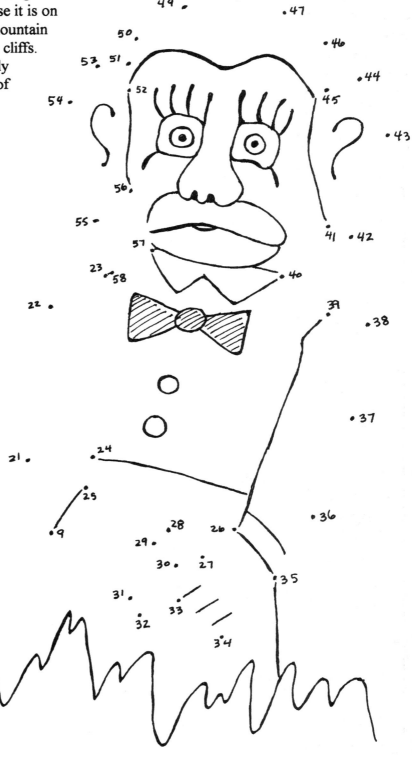

Los nombres en Espanol en Nuevo Mejico (Spanish names in New Mexico)

The Spanish settlers who came to New Mexico brought many things with them. They taught the Pueblo people to build outdoor mud ovens called hornos. You can still see hornos at many pueblos today. They also taught the native people how to make beautiful jewelry and decorations from silver.

The Spanish also gave names to hundreds of places in New Mexico. Those names are still used today. Below is a wordfind of Spanish place names in New Mexico. See how many you can find.

```
E A G U A F R I A W K
M M P E C O S Z Z C F
B U O T A F E B U O A
U Z T R B V N E L V L
D E S P A N O L A R G
O T V H L K G E L E O
A N C X L Y A N A U D
C O V W O B L A N C O
A M A S O R A L U T Ñ
B X D P T D D U L C E
K A O V O R R O C O S
```

Agua Fria
Algodones
Baca
Belen
Blanco
Caballo
Chavez
Cuervo
Dulce
Embudo
Espanola
La Luz
Luna
Montezuma
Mora
Nogal
Pecos
Socorro
Tularosa
Vado

Un poquito Espanol (oon po-KEE-to es-pan-YOLE)

Here's a short Spanish lesson for you:

Buenos dias (way-nos DEE-us) - Good day.
Holla (ho-LAH) - Hello.
Que paso? (kay PAH-so) - What's happening?
Nada (NAH-duh) - Nothing.
Por favor (pore fuh-VORE) - Please.
Gracias (GRAH-see-us) - Thank you.
Habla Espanol? (ah-blah es-pan-YOLE) - Do you speak Spanish?
Un poquito (oon po-KEE-to) - A little.
Si (SEE) - Yes. No (you know how to say this one) - No.
Este chile es muy caliente (ES-tay CHEE-lay ess MOO-y cal-ee-EN-tay) - This chile is very hot.
Que este haciendo aqui este pajaro tonto? (kay es-tay ha-see-EN-do ah-KEE es-tay pah-HA-ro TON-to) - What's this stupid bird doing here?

WHEW! THIS IS HARD!

From Mexico to the United States

For many years, the land we now call New Mexico was owned by Spain. Then in 1821, the Spanish settlers and native Americans rebelled against Spain and started a new country -- Mexico. Much of what is now the southwestern part of the United States was then part of Mexico. But settlers also began to come into this country from the United States. In 1846, the United States went to war against Mexico and took New Mexico from them. It then became a territory of the United States.

Not everyone in New Mexico wanted to be part of the United States. One group of settlers and Indians were so unhappy about being Americans that they murdered the first American governor!

The Long Walk

The Pueblo people and the Spanish and American settlers were not the only people in New Mexico. Navajos (NAH-vuh-hose) and Apaches (uh-PA-chees) lived here, too. They sometimes raided the pueblos and the Spanish settlements and stole food and other things. The Navajos and Apaches believed they had a right to take things from the settlers, because the settlers were taking their land. The United States army began to kill the Indians to protect the settlers. Finally, they forced the native people to march hundreds of miles on foot to a camp at Bosque Redondo near Fort Sumner. This march is know as the Long Walk. Many of the people died of hunger or exhaustion on the way. Many more died in the camp from disease.

The Navajos and Apaches hated living together in a small place. The land at Bosque Redondo was bad for crops, and the Apaches didn't know how to farm. After two years, the Apaches escaped. One group of Apaches, the Mescaleros (mess-cuh-LAIR-ohs), were finally given some land for a reservation in the Sacramento Mountains near Ruidoso. Another group of Apaches, the Jicarillas (hick-uh-REE-yuhs), were given land for a reservation in northern New Mexico.

A few years later, the Navajos were allowed to return to their homeland in western New Mexico and eastern Arizona. The Navajo reservation is the largest Indian reservation in the United States.

Kit Carson

Kit Carson was one of the famous "mountain men" of the west. When he was a teenager in Missouri, he boarded a wagon train passing through. When the train stopped in Taos, New Mexico, Carson got off. He became a fur trapper, Indian fighter, and guide, living in the Rocky Mountains.

Kit Carson was a hero to the settlers because he helped protect them from the Indians. Some people say that Carson respected the native people, even though he often fought them. But he was never a hero to the Navajos and Apaches.

Kit Carson's home in Taos is now a museum. Visitors to the museum can see how early New Mexico settlers lived.

You can see the Bosque Redondo reservation and learn more about the Long Walk at Fort Sumner State Monument just south of Fort Sumner.

I found Fort Sumner on the map! (5-D)

The Santa Fe Trail

The first people to come to the territory of New Mexico from the United States were traders. They brought wagons full of pots, tools, cloth, spices, and other goods to the Spanish settlers. In trade, they took home furs, gold, and silver. The wagons, pulled by mules or oxen, travelled a trail that stretched from Kansas City to Santa Fe. It was called the Santa Fe Trail.

The traders and trappers who travelled the Santa Fe Trail were often attacked by Indians. The United States army set up forts to protect the travellers. When the Indians were moved onto reservations, settlers also began to come into the territory along the trail. The Santa Fe Trail was the most important route into New Mexico for almost a hundred years. There are still some ruts from the wagon wheels in the prairies of eastern New Mexico.

At the Aztec Museum Pioneer Village in Aztec, you can see how the pioneers lived. Some of the objects below are things the pioneers used. Some are definitely not! Circle all the things you think the pioneers would have used when they settled in New Mexico. Put a big X over the things you think they would NOT have used.

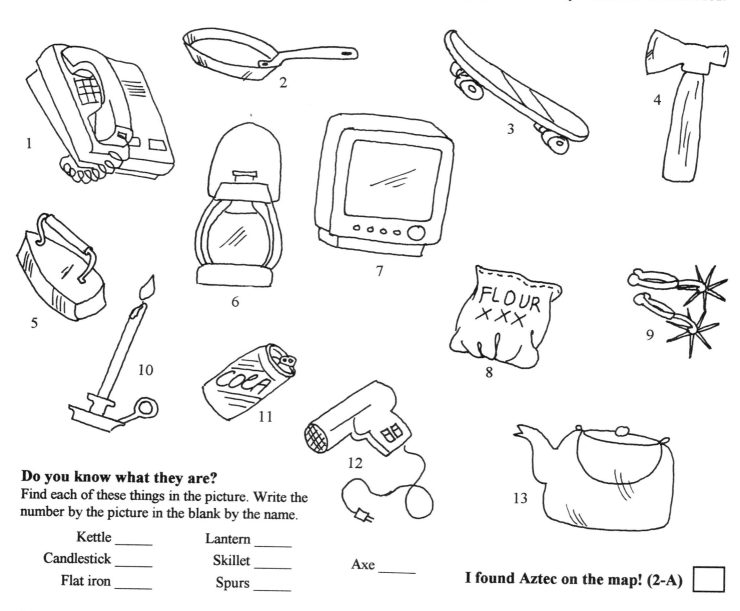

Do you know what they are?
Find each of these things in the picture. Write the number by the picture in the blank by the name.

Kettle _____   Lantern _____

Candlestick _____   Skillet _____   Axe _____

Flat iron _____   Spurs _____   **I found Aztec on the map! (2-A)** ☐

Learn more about New Mexico pioneer life by visiting El Rancho de las Golondrinas, a living museum at La Cienega near Santa Fe, and at Shakespeare, a ghost town near Lordsburg.

Ghosts and ghost towns

Visitors to New Mexico territory soon became greedy for the valuable gold and silver they found in the mountains. Miners began to rush into the territory by the thousands. They built dozens of small towns near the mines. When the silver and gold was all mined out, the towns were often abandoned. Ghost towns of empty homes and stores were left behind.

Many people like to visit old ghost towns. This map shows where to find some of New Mexico's ghost towns. Which of the trails goes to all ten of the towns? Write your answer on the line below the map.

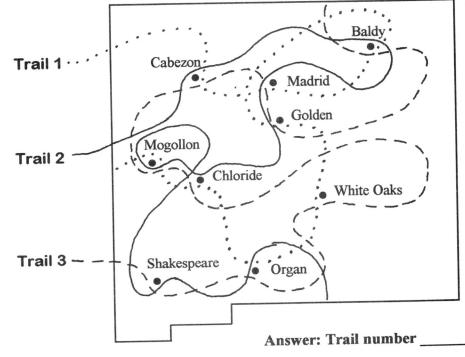

Answer: Trail number _____

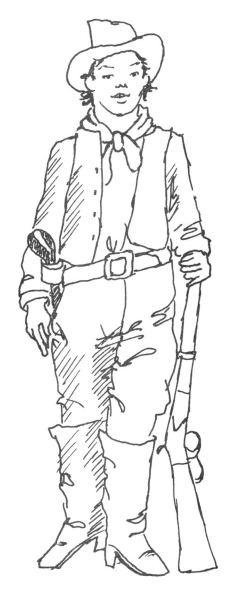

New Mexico territory was sometimes a rough and lawless land. Train robbers, rustlers, and other outlaws roamed the territory and hid out in the hills and mountains. Homesteaders, cattlemen, and miners often fought bitter wars for control of the country. A famous range war was fought in New Mexico. It was the Lincoln County War. It started with a feud between two shop owners in the town of Lincoln. Soon farmers and ranchers joined the battle. Outlaws from all over the territory were hired to fight for both sides. Many people were killed.

One of the most famous outlaws to fight in the Lincoln County War was a young man named Henry McCarty. Henry was born in New York City, and moved to New Mexico when he was 14 years old. When he came to New Mexico, he changed his name to William Antrim. William was in and out of jail for burglary and other crimes most of his life. He killed a guard while escaping from the Lincoln County jail. Finally, in 1881 when he was 21 years old, he was shot and killed by Sheriff Pat Garrett. William had a famous nickname. Do you know what it is? Unscramble the letters to read it.

Learn more about William Antrim and the Lincoln County war at the Historical Museum in the town of Lincoln.

I found Lincoln on the map! (4-E) ☐

LIBLY   ETH   IKD

_ _ _ _ _   _ _ _   _ _ _

15

The Forty-seventh state

In 1912, New Mexico became the 47th state of the United States of America. New Mexico's state capital city is the oldest and highest state capital in the United States.

Below are some paragraphs that describe New Mexico's capital city. Each paragraph contains a word printed in **BOLD** print. Fit that word into a space in the puzzle below. (Two letters have been done to help you get started.) When all the words are in place, unscramble the letters in the boxes to spell the name of New Mexico's state capital. Write it on the lines below the puzzle.

The **PLAZA** is a square formed by streets in the center of town. In the many shops around the plaza, you can buy postcards, cowboy boots and hats, Christmas tree lights that look like chile peppers, and lots of other things.

Almost all of the buildings in the city are made of **ADOBE.** Bricks made of sand, straw, and mud form the walls. Roofs are made of vigas (VEE-guz), which are logs. Everything is covered with a mud plaster. Window sills and doors are often painted turquoise for good luck.

The **PALACE OF THE GOVERNORS** was built by the Spanish nearly 400 years ago. The Palace is now a historical museum. You can see ancient Indian pottery or a pioneer chuck wagon, and learn more about New Mexico and its fascinating past.

Every day in front of the Palace of the Governors, Native Americans sell their beautiful handmade jewelry and other crafts at the **INDIAN MARKET.**

A big celebration called **FIESTA** celebrates the return of the Spanish after the Pueblo revolt. Read about the Pueblo revolt and Fiesta on page 9.

There is a beautiful outdoor **OPERA** theater in this city. Famous singers and musicians from all over the world perform here every summer.

At Christmas, many homes and buildings are decorated with **LUMINARIAS** (loo-min-AH-ree-uhz). Brown paper bags are filled with sand and a candle is stuck into the sand. They are place around the roofs of buildings, and along sidewalks and fences.

New Mexico's state capital is ____ ____ ____ ____ ____   ____ ____

Now that you know the name of the capital city, see if you can find it on the map *without using coordinates!* When you find it, write the coordinates in the blank spaces below. Here are some hints: Look for the name in the north central part of the state. It is northeast of Albuquerque. It is marked with a star.

I found New Mexico's state capital on the map! (The coordinates are ___ , ___)

Fiesta!

Every September, Santa Fe is host to the oldest community celebration in the United States. This Fiesta has parades, fireworks, music, dancing, and food. It also has a special parade just for kids. It's the Children's Pet Parade. Some kids bring their pets, and some dress as pets! Can you find all of the 17 animals in this picture of the Children's Pet Parade?

More things to see and do in Santa Fe...

The Santa Fe Children's Museum has lots of hands-on activities and art and science projects for kids. Storytellers, magicians, and live animals add to the fun.

The La Fonda Hotel has been around since cowboys rode in on the Santa Fe Trail. Some say Billy the Kid was once a dishwasher here. Look around the old adobe building to get an idea of what a hotel was like in the last century.

Wheelwright Museum is a huge hogan, like the ones the Navajos live in. Downstairs is an old reservation trading post. This is a great place to learn about the Navajo people.

More cool places to go: The Museum of International Folk Art, the Museum of Indian Arts and Culture, and the Randall Davey Audubon Center.

The Santa Fe Indian Market

The Indians of New Mexico are world famous for their arts and crafts. Native American artists and craftspeople line the streets of Santa Fe's Plaza every weekend. A special two-day Indian Market is held every August. Prizes are given for the best works of art displayed during these two days. Paintings, sculpture, pottery, jewelry, and other crafts are displayed during the Market.

Below are some examples of art you might see during Indian Market. You can color these examples. Colored pencils will work best, but you can also use crayons.

The Zuni people carve animals, called fetishes, from stone. They often tie an arrowhead and some feathers on the animal's back. The Zuni believe the fetishes help bring good luck to hunters.

A Cochiti craftswoman made the first clay storyteller. Now storyteller figures are very popular in the Southwest.

Silver and turquoise jewelry is made by Navajos and by Pueblo people. This design is called a "squash blossom" because it looks like the flowers on squash vines.

Indian pottery is made without a potter's wheel. The potter makes long ropes of clay. The ropes are coiled around to make a pot shape. After the clay is smoothed out, it is fired in an outdoor oven to make it hard. Then the potter paints the design on the pot with a brush or with a yucca leaf.

Kachina Dolls

Kachinas are dancers who represent the spirits of the Hopi and Zuni people. Dolls are carved from wood to look like the Kachinas. Then they are painted and decorated with feathers. The dolls are given to young children of the tribe to help teach them about the spirits.

Kachina dolls are sold in many shops in Santa Fe and other New Mexico towns. If your parents decide to buy a Kachina doll, tell them to be sure it was made by a Native American.

Qaokatsina is a Corn Kachina. He gives the people sacred corn to plant for the coming season.

Tawakatsina is the Sun Spirit. He is gentle and kind, and is a very sacred Kachina. He is not often seen in the ceremonial dances.

This is a flat "crib" kachina doll. These dolls were given to infants. This Kachina is Hanomana, a Hopi maiden.

The kids of New Mexico's pueblos

Thousands of kids live in the pueblos of New Mexico. They do the same things you do. Most of the time, they dress like you, too. But when their pueblo has a special feast day or ceremonial, they sometimes dress in traditional clothes. Each ceremonial has special clothes. Kids taking part in the ceremonials may paint their skin and wear feathers and bells. You can visit the pueblos to see some of these ceremonials, or you can see them at the Indian Pueblo Cultural Center in Albuquerque.

Can you guess which dancer is which? Write the dancer's number in the space by the name.

Buffalo Dancer _____

Rainbow Dancer _____

Harvest Dancer _____

Butterfly Dancer _____

When you visit a pueblo...
Remember, you are a guest here. Use your best manners. Respect the privacy and customs of the Pueblo people. When you watch ceremonial dances, don't applaud or talk to the dancers. Pointing is considered very rude. Carry out everything you bring in (soda cans, trash) or put it into a trash can. Be quiet (don't yell or run through the pueblo.) If you want to take a picture of someone, ask first. Always ask before you enter a home or building.

New Mexico's Pueblos

Acoma
Cochiti
Isleta
Jemez
Laguna
Nambe
Picuris
Pojoaque
Sandia
San Felipe
San Ildefonso
San Juan
Santa Ana
Santa Clara
Santo Domingo
Taos
Tesuque
Zia
Zuni

These beautiful handpainted headdresses are called tablitas (tab-LEE-tuhs).

Connect the dots to draw a picture of Taos Pueblo, New Mexico's most famous pueblo. People have lived in the Taos Pueblo area for at least a thousand years. The round shape in front of the pueblo is an outdoor oven called a horno. Spanish settlers taught the Taos people to build and use these ovens. Pueblo women still bake traditional Indian bread in the hornos. You can often buy this delicious bread at Taos and other New Mexico pueblos.

Living on the Navajo Reservation

New Mexico's part of the huge Navajo Reservation is in the northwest corner of the state. It includes the "Four Corners" area, the only place in the United States where four state borders join in a perfect cross shape. Across the border in the Arizona part of the reservation is Monument Valley, a Navajo tribal park open to the public. It has some of the most beautiful scenery in the United States. Many western movies have been filmed in Monument Valley.

Before they were moved onto the reservation, the Navajo people were nomads. Nomads are people who move from place to place to find food and shelter. Wherever they stayed, the Navajos built hogans (a Navajo word that means home). Hogans are houses made of logs or mud. They usually have six or eight sides. A fireplace is built in the center of the hogan, and a hole in the roof lets the smoke out.

Many Navajos now make their living by raising sheep and goats. Some Navajos still live in hogans, but many have more modern houses. Some families have both. Because their homes are far apart, Navajo children often must ride a bus for hours to go to school.

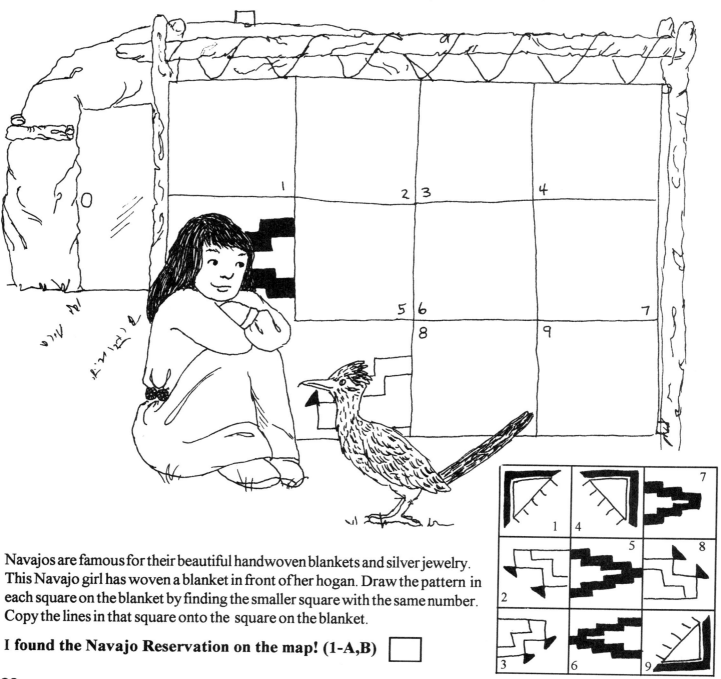

Navajos are famous for their beautiful handwoven blankets and silver jewelry. This Navajo girl has woven a blanket in front of her hogan. Draw the pattern in each square on the blanket by finding the smaller square with the same number. Copy the lines in that square onto the square on the blanket.

I found the Navajo Reservation on the map! (1-A,B) ☐

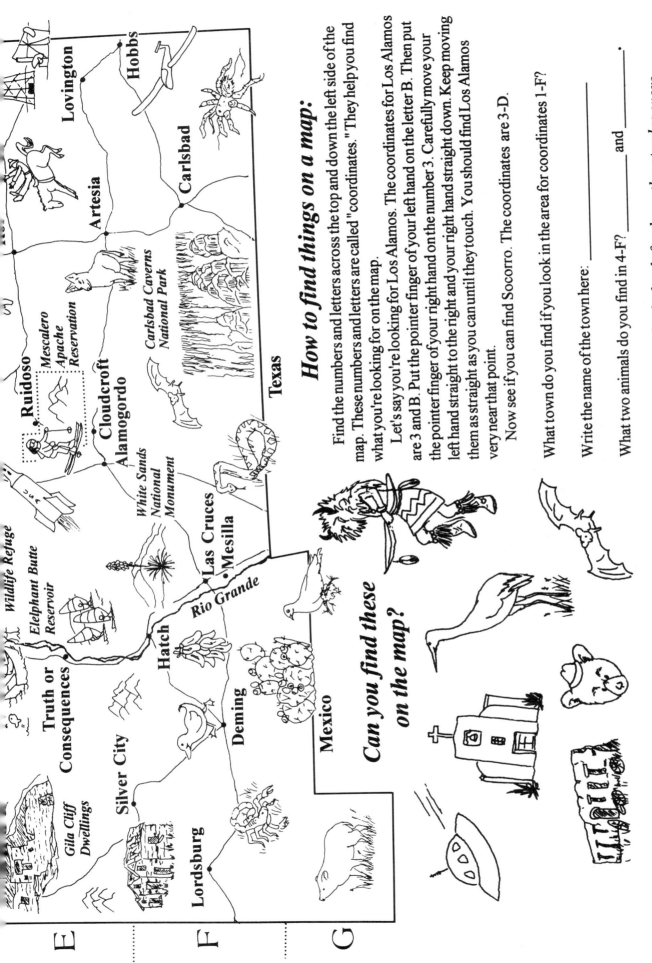

How to find things on a map:

Find the numbers and letters across the top and down the left side of the map. These numbers and letters are called "coordinates." They help you find what you're looking for on the map.

Let's say you're looking for Los Alamos. The coordinates for Los Alamos are 3 and B. Put the pointer finger of your left hand on the letter B. Then put the pointer finger of your right hand on the number 3. Carefully move your left hand straight to the right and your right hand straight down. Keep moving them as straight as you can until they touch. You should find Los Alamos very near that point.

Now see if you can find Socorro. The coordinates are 3-D.

What town do you find if you look in the area for coordinates 1-F?

Write the name of the town here: _____

What two animals do you find in 4-F? _____ and _____.

Carefully pull the map out of the book. Then put a little clear tape over the holes left where the staples were.

Can you find these on the map?

Texas

Mexico

Rio Grande

Truth or Consequences
Silver City
Lordsburg
Deming
Hatch
Las Cruces
Mesilla

Gila Cliff Dwellings
Elelphant Butte Reservoir
Wildlife Refuge

White Sands National Monument
Alamogordo
Cloudcroft
Ruidoso
Mescalero Apache Reservation
Carlsbad Caverns National Park

Artesia
Carlsbad
Lovington
Hobbs

E
F
G

The Big Chile Chase

You're going after the Big Chile! Here's what you'll need: Three coins that have heads and tails, and a playing piece fo[r] each player (a button, a bottle cap, a rock, or anything about that size.) Let each player choose a playing piece. Then put them all into a can or hat or any container you can find. Draw them out one at a time to decide what order you'll play in. (first playing piece drawn plays first, and so on.) When it's your turn, shake the three coins in your hand. The[n] drop them onto the game board. Move your playing piece one space for each coin that shows heads. (Three heads, move three spaces; two heads and one tail, move two spaces; one head and two tails, move one space; three tails, st[ay] where you are.) If the space you land on has a message, do what it tells you to do (or lose a turn!). If you land on a space with a chile, hop around in a circle on one foot. With each hop, say "Yieee!" and fan your mouth with both hand[s]. First player to reach the Big Chile wins the game. The game starts at the top of the next page.

Your duck Dilbert wins the Deming Duck Race - go ahead three spaces.

Make a face like Zozobra

Hey! It's me!

You eat too many chiles - go back to the beginning.

Put one hand on something red. Keep it there 'til your next turn. If you move it too soon, miss a turn.

Sail ahead two spaces on Elephant Butte Lake.

DO NOT SMILE until your next turn. If you do, miss a turn.

You go to the Portales Peanut Festival. Miss a turn.

You get lost in Carlsbad Caverns. Miss two turns.

Start here, Amigos!

Whistle (or sing) "Happy Birthday."

Put a sock on your head. Leave it there for the rest of the game.

You go for a balloon ride. Miss one turn.

...ide the ...andia ...ram ...head ...ne ...pace.

You get sand in your underwear at White Sands. Miss a turn.

Say "Chunky Chile, Cactus Cheesecake" three times as fast as you can.

You find an agate at Rock Hound State Park. Go ahead two spaces.

You break your leg skiing at Angel Fire. Go back two spaces.

NEW MEXICO

Texas

Colorado

Arizona

Rio Grande

	1	2	3	4	5	6
A	Shiprock, Navajo Reservation	Aztec, Farmington, Jicarilla Apache Reservation	Chama	Red River, Eagle Nest	Raton	Capulin Volcano National Monument, Clayton
B	Gallup, Zuni Pueblo, Red Rock State Park	Grants, El Morro National Monument	Los Alamos, Espanola, Bandelier National Monument	Taos, Cimarron	Cimarron, Fort Union National Monument	
C		Acoma Pueblo	Belen, Albuquerque	Santa Fe, Pecos	Las Vegas	Tucumcari, Santa Rosa, Vaughn
D		National Radio Astronomy Observatory	Socorro			Clovis, Fort Sumner, Portales, Smokey Bear

Growing up Apache

Fit each of the words in **boldface type** in the paragraphs below into the crossword puzzle. Count the number of letters in the word. Then find the space in the crossword that fits the word. A couple of letters have been filled in to get you started. (HINT: Fill in the <u>longest</u> words first.)

This **Jicarilla** boy is running in a ceremonial **relay** race. The race is part of a three-day camp the Jicarilla have each year near Dulce. Two teams take part in the race. They are members of the two bands of Jicarilla Apaches. The **Ollero** band represents animals and sun, and its color is white. The **Llanero** band represents plants and the moon, and its color is **red**. Many of the Jicarillas live in tipis during the **camp.**

I found the Jicarilla Reservation on the map! (3-A)

Every Fourth of **July,** the **Mescalero** Apaches have a puberty **ceremonial** for Apache girls who have become women that year. The Sunrise Ceremony lasts for four **days** and four nights. The girls wear beautiful hand-sewn leather dresses decorated with beads and **feathers.** They dance each night to the singing of Apache boys and men.

I found the Mescalero Reservation on the map! (4-E)

The Cumbres and Toltec Railroad

The historic old Cumbres and Toltec Railroad passenger train starts its ride in Chama, New Mexico. It travels over narrow-gauge rails across Cumbres Pass, which is over 10,000 feet high. The mountain scenery along the route is spectacular, and the dropoffs are hair-raising! Passengers can ride all the way into Colorado, with a stop for lunch in the mountains. See if you can find the 8 differences between these two drawings of the Cumbres and Toltec Engine.

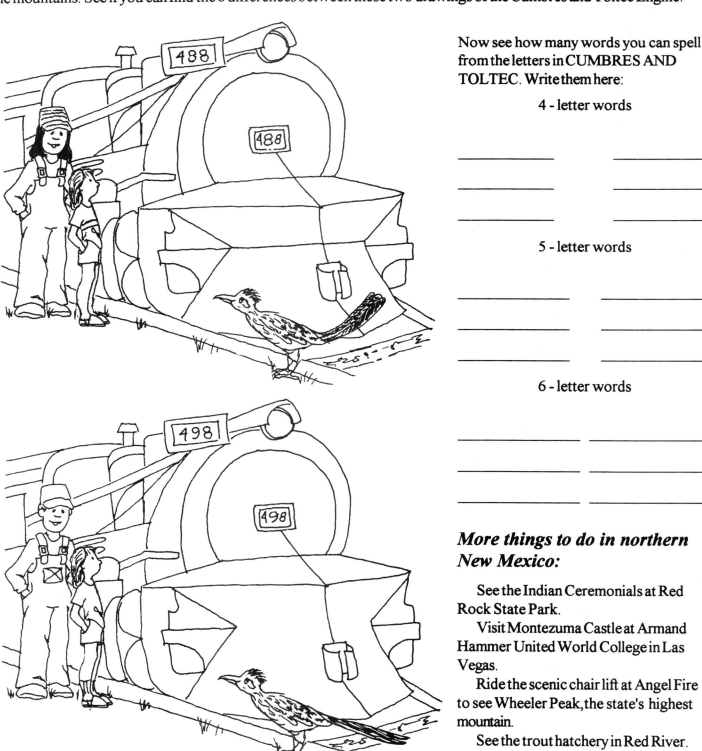

I found Chama (3-A) on the map! ☐

Now see how many words you can spell from the letters in CUMBRES AND TOLTEC. Write them here:

4 - letter words

_____   _____

_____   _____

_____   _____

5 - letter words

_____   _____

_____   _____

_____   _____

6 - letter words

_____   _____

_____   _____

_____   _____

More things to do in northern New Mexico:

See the Indian Ceremonials at Red Rock State Park.

Visit Montezuma Castle at Armand Hammer United World College in Las Vegas.

Ride the scenic chair lift at Angel Fire to see Wheeler Peak, the state's highest mountain.

See the trout hatchery in Red River.

Look down at the river from the Rio Grand Gorge Bridge.

Proud descendents of the Spanish settlers

Many New Mexicans are descendents of the first European settlers who travelled north from Mexico on the Camino Real. Some have lived in New Mexico all their lives. Some moved here from Mexico. They are called Hispanic, or Chicano, or Latino. Most of them speak Spanish as well as English. Use the code at the right to decode the words below and find out more about these fascinating people.

The first cowboys were Spanish __ __ __ __ __ __ __ __. They herded cattle on horse-
22 1 17 21 5 18 15 19

back. Nowdays, many Hispanics like to ride in their __ __ __ __ __ __ __ __ __, cars
12 15 23 18 9 4 5 18 19

that are painted with fancy designs. Most Hispanics like to listen to traditional Mexican music, called

__ __ __ __ __ __ __ __, and to modern __ __ __ __ __ __ __ __ and
13 1 18 9 1 3 8 9   18 1 14 3 8 5 18 1

__ __ __ __ __. This music is played during __ __ __ __ __ __ __ in Mesilla and
19 1 12 19 1   6 9 5 19 20 1 19

Espanola. Delicious Mexican food, like __ __ __ __ __ __ __, are popular in New Mexico.
20 1 13 1 12 5 19

The town of __ __ __ __ __ __ __ is famous for the many Hispanic weavers who live and
3 8 9 13 1 25 15

work there, making beautiful handwoven __ __ __ __ __ __ __ __.
2 12 1 14 11 5 20 19

This is a picture of a santo (saint). A religious painting is

called a __ __ __ __ __ __ __.
18 5 20 1 2 12 15

A religious carving is a __ __ __ __ __.
2 21 12 20 15

Artists who make religious paintings or carvings

are called __ __ __ __ __ __ __ __ __.
19 1 14 20 5 18 15 19

Hispanic artists also make beautiful objects from

__ __ __ __ __ __ and __ __ __.
19 9 12 22 5 18   20 9 14

Many woodcarvers live and work in the town of

__ __ __ __ __ __ __. Hispanic artists show
3 15 18 4 15 22 1

their work every year at the Traditional Spanish

__ __ __ __ __ __ in Santa Fe. There is a
13 1 18 11 5 20

special category for young artists under 18 years old.

A good place to learn more about New Mexico's Hispanic people is at the Palace of the Governors in Santa Fe.

A	1
B	2
C	3
D	4
E	5
F	6
G	7
H	8
I	9
J	10
K	11
L	12
M	13
N	14
O	15
P	16
Q	17
R	18
S	19
T	20
U	21
V	22
W	23
X	24
Y	25
Z	26

The Duke City

New Mexico's largest city was named for the Duke of Alburquerque, an important Spanish nobleman. Over the years, the first "r" in his name was dropped to make the name Albuquerque (AL-buh-ker-kee). Since it was named for a duke, Albuquerque is called the Duke City.

The clear blue skies and warm air over Albuquerque make it a perfect place to fly hot air balloons. Every year, the world's largest hot air balloon rally is held here. Hundreds of balloons fill the sky every morning.

Which two of these balloons have exactly the same design?

I found Albuquerque on the map! (3-C)

Find your way around Albuquerque

Albuquerque is full of fun things to see and do. Find the route below that will take you to each of these nine great Albuquerque places.

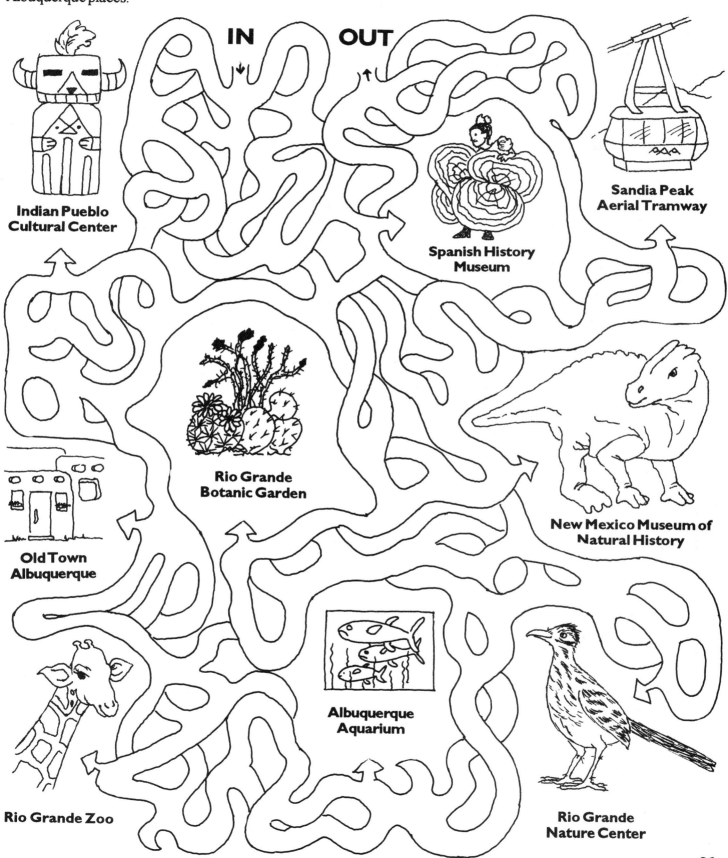

IN

OUT

Indian Pueblo Cultural Center

Spanish History Museum

Sandia Peak Aerial Tramway

Rio Grande Botanic Garden

Old Town Albuquerque

New Mexico Museum of Natural History

Rio Grande Zoo

Albuquerque Aquarium

Rio Grande Nature Center

Moonwalkers, stargazers, and rocket makers

A lot of really smart people live and work in New Mexico. They study outer space (and sometimes fly into it). They make computer parts and build weapons. They also find ways to use atomic and solar energy to make electricity and to treat people who are sick.

Can you match each picture on these two pages with the paragraph that describes it? Put the number by the picture in the space by the paragraph.

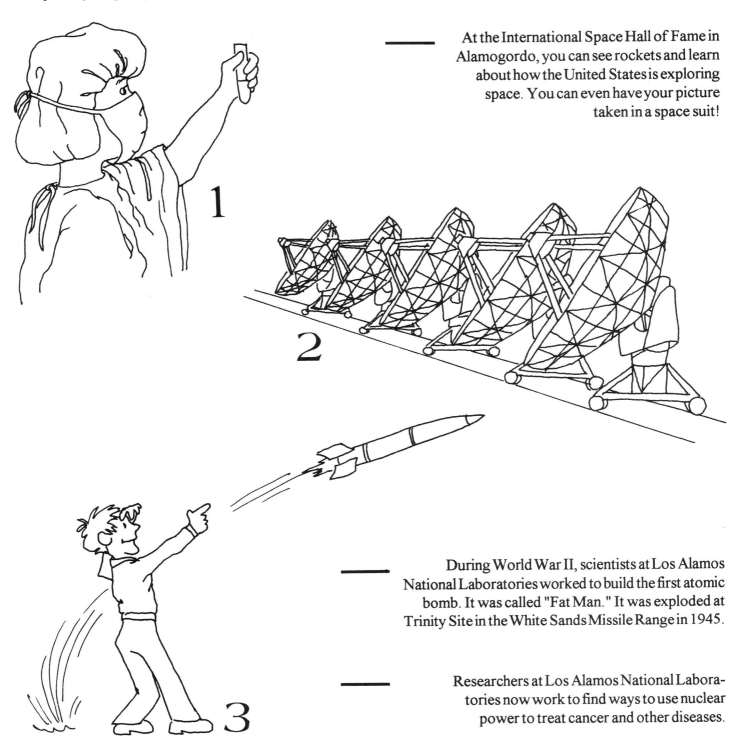

_____ At the International Space Hall of Fame in Alamogordo, you can see rockets and learn about how the United States is exploring space. You can even have your picture taken in a space suit!

_____ During World War II, scientists at Los Alamos National Laboratories worked to build the first atomic bomb. It was called "Fat Man." It was exploded at Trinity Site in the White Sands Missile Range in 1945.

_____ Researchers at Los Alamos National Laboratories now work to find ways to use nuclear power to treat cancer and other diseases.

4

5

6

_____ Robert Goddard built the first liquid fuel rocket at his laboratory near Roswell. You can see some of his rockets and the instruments he used to build them at the Goddard Museum in Roswell.

_____ The Very Large Array is a group of 27 radio telescopes that move on tracks on the plains near Socorro. Together, these telescopes form the largest radio telescope in the world. Radio telescopes listen to sounds from outer space.

_____ Astronomers study the sun at the Sacramento Peak Observatory near Sunspot. They use the world's largest coronagraph, a special kind of telescope, to study the sun's flares and sunspots. At the Apache Point Observatory, they can look at other stars and galaxies.

Picture this!

There's a lot to see and do in southern and eastern New Mexico. Use the clues below to complete the crossword puzzle and learn more about this part of the state. The pictures on the next page will help you solve the clues. There is a picture for each word in the puzzle.

ACROSS

1 - In 1947, something crashed on a ranch near Roswell. Some people believe that it was an alien spacecraft, or "flying ___ ___ ___ ___ ___ ___."

3 - If you like hot, spicy food, you don't want to miss the ___ ___ ___ ___ ___ Festival in Hatch.

4 - You're probably wearing clothes made from this plant that grows on farms in the southern and eastern parts of the state.

6 - You can see hundreds of these pumping away on the plains of eastern New Mexico.

7 - If you have one of these, enter it in the annual Deming ___ ___ ___ ___ Race.

9 - Portales has a festival each year to honor these tasty little treats that grow on its farmlands.

DOWN

2 - You can munch away on one of these at the Hillsboro ___ ___ ___ ___ ___ Festival.

3 - Ranchers raise thousands of these in New Mexico.

4 - Silver City and Lincoln both have an annual ___ ___ ___ ___ ___ ___ Poetry and Music Festival.

5 - You can find agates, crystals, and other special things at ___ ___ ___ ___ Hound State Park near Deming.

8 - New Mexico dairy farmers raise the cows that give the milk that this is made from.

GOT any Peanuts?

YIKES!

Was it really a UFO?

Most people think that what crashed near Roswell was really an American experimental aircraft. But nobody seems to know for sure. You can find out more about the crash at the International UFO Museum and Research Center in Roswell.

Two very special New Mexico places

White Sands National Monument is the largest gypsum sand dune field in the world, and it is REALLY FUN to see and play in. The dunes get up to 60 feet high. They're a great place for rolling or sliding down on a piece of cardboard. All this sand comes from the mountains around White Sands. Rain dissolves the gypsum in the mountains. The rain water gets trapped in a big basin between the mountains. When the water evaporates, gypsum crystals are left behind. Wind breaks the crystals into tiny bits of sand. Then it blows them into dunes. New sand is being made all the time. So don't worry if you carry some home in your clothes - and you will! Be sure to take some sunscreen with you when you go. The white sand reflects sunlight and makes it even hotter and more likely to cause sunburn. Keep plenty of water handy, too. You'll be glad you have it! White Sands is near Alamogordo.

TAKE THESE WITH YOU:

Lots of WATER!   SUN SCREEN   SUN GLASSES   VISOR   STUFF TO DIG SAND WITH   SNACKS   BAG TO CARRY TRASH OUT

SPF 15

New Mexico's other very special place is **Carlsbad Caverns National Park.** These huge caves were also made by water. Millions of years ago, there was a huge sea in this part of New Mexico. When the sea dried up, the mud that was left behind became limestone. Hundreds of thousands of years ago, water began to trickle into cracks in this limestone. Very slowly, it dissolved the limestone and left behind these enormous caves. They are filled with stalactites and stalagmites, strange forms made from the limestone. Stalagmites grow up from the floor, and stalactites grow down from the ceiling. Sometimes they meet, making a column. Many of the formations in Carlsbad Caverns have names, like Whale's Mouth, Lion's Tail, and Twin Domes. There are several rooms in the caverns with names like King's Palace and Dome Room.

It takes a whole day to see Carlsbad Caverns. Don't bother to take your lunch with you - it's more fun to get a box lunch in the lunchroom inside the caverns. Take a sweater, because it's always cool inside the caverns - even in the middle of the summer when it's really hot outside. And wear shoes with good traction. The caverns are damp and the walkways are slippery. ALWAYS stay on the path, and don't touch the formations.

Carlsbad Caverns' furry residents

Just before sunset on summer evenings, you'll see something really neat outside the entrance to Carlsbad Caverns. It looks like a big cloud of smoke coming from the caverns. But it's really thousands of bats that live in the caves, coming out to look for bugs to eat during the night. The bats sleep in one of the rooms, called Bat Cave, during the day. They hang upside down from the ceiling of the cave. That way, they can stay close together and keep each other warm. You can't go into Bat Cave to see them. Only scientists are allowed in Bat Cave, so the bats won't be disturbed. Bats are shy animals, and they are not dangerous to people. They are really very fascinating. Bats eat about half their own weight in food every night. They use echolocation to find bugs to eat and branches to duck in the dark. Echolocation works sort of like radar. The bats make very high-pitched squeaks, and the sound bounces back at them from objects around them. That's why they have such big ears -- so they can hear the "echoes" of the squeaks they make. These echoes tell them how close the object is, and whether it is something to eat or stay away from.

This little bat needs some help finding her way back to Bat Cave. Can you get her there?

I found White Sands (3 and 4-F) and Carlsbad Caverns (4 and 5-F) on the map!

New Mexico's unique wildlife

All kinds of wild critters live in New Mexico--squirrels, skunks, deer, raccoons, lizards, porcupines, and many, many more. Here are just a few of New Mexico's most special animals. Unscramble the letters to spell each animal's name. Put a check mark in the box by each animal you see in New Mexico.

These graceful and swift animals are sometimes called antelope, but they really aren't. They are found in the US southwest, and nowhere else on earth. They are the fastest wild animals in America. Some can run as fast as fifty miles an hour. These animals also have excellent eyesight. They can see as well as a human looking through binoculars. The markings on their chests are like fingerprints--no two animals have the same markings.

gronnhorp   __ __ __ __ __ __ __ __ __

The big ears of these desert animals act like heat radiators to help keep them cool in the hot summer days.

brackbajit

__ __ __ __ __ __ __ __ __ __

You may see some of these animals from the highway as you drive through New Mexico. You can also see them and other New Mexico wildlife at Living Desert State Park near Carlsbad and at zoos in most cities.

These animals are sometimes seen in the mountains of New Mexico. A young one found orphaned after a forest fire became the mascot of the US Forest Service.

clabk rabe

__ __ __ __ __   __ __ __ __

Some say this animal sings. It was held in such reverence by Native Americans that they would not hunt or kill it. It was believed to have magical powers and to bring good luck. It was also sometimes called "the trickster."

toycoe __ __ __ __ __ __

These cute little animals live in underground burrows in communities called "towns." You might spot one out on the plains of New Mexico, watching you from a safe distance. You can also see them in most of New Mexico's zoos.

riperia dgo __ __ __ __ __ __ __   __ __ __

Birds of New Mexico

Hundreds of different kinds of birds live in New Mexico. Some of them are birds of prey, or predators (PRED-uh-ters). Predators have sharp bills and powerful claws to help them catch and eat small animals like mice and lizards. They also have sharp eyesight and large, powerful wings.

Look at each of the birds on these two pages. Can you tell which ones are predators? Put a check mark in the box by each bird you think is a predator. Use the color guides to color all the birds.

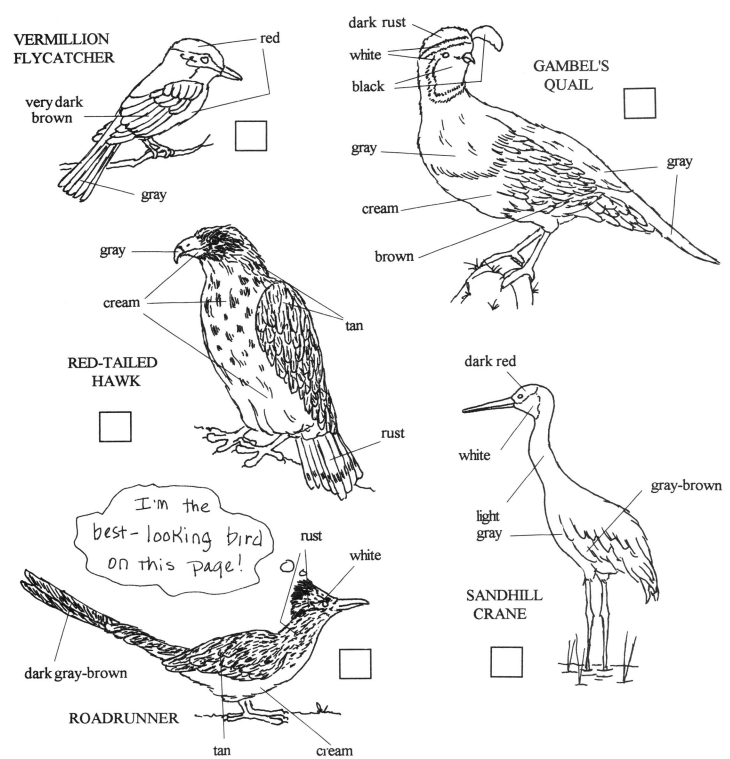

VERMILLION FLYCATCHER — red — very dark brown — gray

GAMBEL'S QUAIL — dark rust — white — black — gray — cream — brown — gray

RED-TAILED HAWK — gray — cream — tan — rust

SANDHILL CRANE — dark red — white — light gray — gray-brown

ROADRUNNER — dark gray-brown — rust — white — tan — cream

I'm the best-looking bird on this page!

yellow

rust

cream

BURROWING
OWL

tan

dark gray

white

gold

black

cream

WESTERN
MEADOWLARK

rust

gold

gray

white

GREAT
HORNED
OWL

tan

cream

gray

SCRUB
JAY

blue

gray

light
gray

blue

dark
gray

black

white

light
gray

BLACK-CHINNED
HUMMINGBIRD

light
gray

MOURNING
DOVE

gray

gray

cream

Creepy-crawlies, New Mexico style

Roadrunner's got to get through this maze of scary critters without running into any of them. Can you help him out?

YOU GOTTA bE KIDDING!

SCORPIONS are small and very poisonous.

TARANTULAS aren't as bad as they look. They do bite, but they're not poisonous.

black yellow Red yellow

GILA MONSTERS are big guys - they grow up to two feet long.

CORAL SNAKES are small but dangerous. Stay away if you see black and red color bands with yellow in between.

I'M OUTTA HERE!

DIAMONDBACK RATTLE-SNAKES give a warning shake of their tails when they feel threatened.

If you see one of these creatures, please don't harm it! Just keep your distance, and it won't bother you.

Fascinating flora

"Flora" means plants, and these plants are especially interesting. Native Americans used them for food, tools, medicine, and even clothes. When you see one of these plants growing in New Mexico, put a check mark in the box next to it.

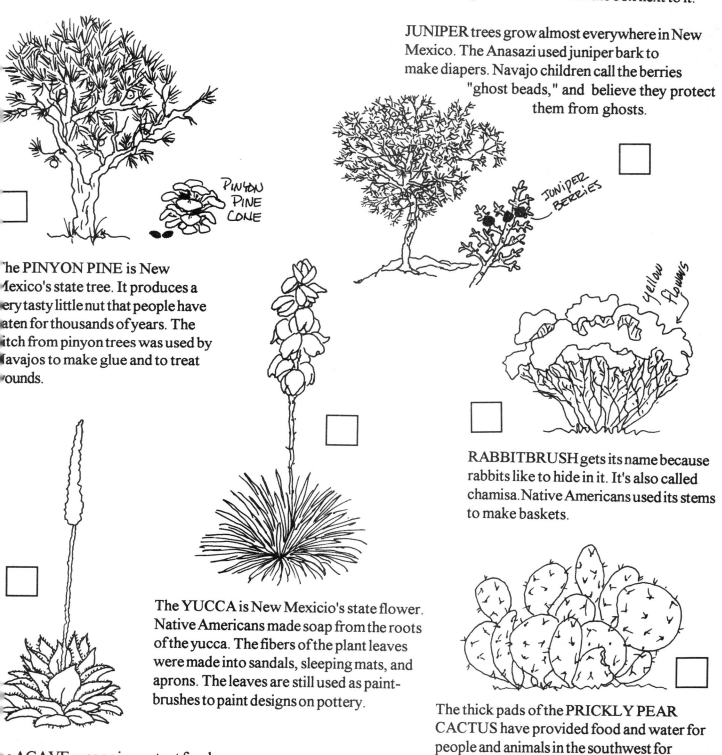

JUNIPER trees grow almost everywhere in New Mexico. The Anasazi used juniper bark to make diapers. Navajo children call the berries "ghost beads," and believe they protect them from ghosts.

PINYON PINE CONE

JUNIPER BERRIES

yellow flowers

The PINYON PINE is New Mexico's state tree. It produces a very tasty little nut that people have eaten for thousands of years. The pitch from pinyon trees was used by Navajos to make glue and to treat wounds.

RABBITBRUSH gets its name because rabbits like to hide in it. It's also called chamisa. Native Americans used its stems to make baskets.

The YUCCA is New Mexicio's state flower. Native Americans made soap from the roots of the yucca. The fibers of the plant leaves were made into sandals, sleeping mats, and aprons. The leaves are still used as paintbrushes to paint designs on pottery.

The thick pads of the PRICKLY PEAR CACTUS have provided food and water for people and animals in the southwest for thousands of years. You can still find them in the produce section of many grocery stores.

The AGAVE was an important food Apaches. It blooms only every ten twenty years.

FTTD* outdoors in New Mexico

New Mexico has many parks, lakes and rivers, hiking and riding trails, camp sites, snowmobile trails, ski runs, and other places for outdoor fun. Look on page 48 for the phone number of the New Mexico Department of Tourism. They will send you free maps that list all the public recreation places in the state. Remember, you need a state license for fishing in public lakes and rivers, and a pueblo license for fishing in pueblo lakes and rivers.

Skiing

Bike riding

Rafting

Fun things to do.

STTR* when you're outdoors in New Mexico

The sun in New Mexico is very bright, even in winter. Always wear sunscreen or sunblock when you're outside for more than a few minutes. In the summer, wear a hat to keep your head cool. Always carry water with you in the summer. Carry a bag to tote out your trash. Leave things the way you find them. Help keep New Mexico beautiful.

Sailing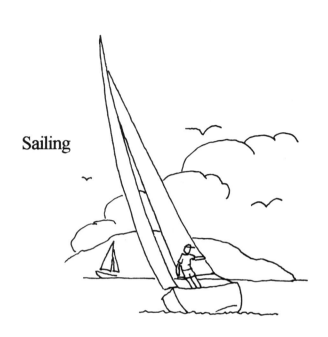

Fishing

 Hiking

Skateboarding

Some things to remember

ANSWERS

Page 2: The roadrunners are on pages 2, 3, 9, 10, 12, 17, 22, 28 (two), 31, 34, 40, 42 (two), 45, 48, on the game, on the map, and on the back cover.

Page 5: writers, race car drivers, hot air balloon, golfer, singer, gymnasts, artists, astronauts, baseball, cartoonists, Pluto.

Page 9:

Page 10:

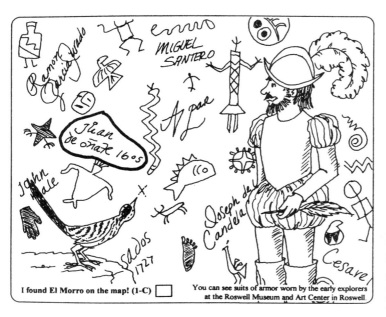

I found El Morro on the map! (1-C) ☐   You can see suits of armor worn by the early explorers at the Roswell Museum and Art Center in Roswell.

Page 11:

Page 12:

Page 14: Pioneers would take the kettle (13), candlestick (10), flat iron (5), lantern (6), skillet (2), spurs (9), axe (4), and the bag of flour.

Page 15: Trail number 3; Billy the Kid.

Page 16: Santa Fe

MORE ANSWERS

Page 17: The animals are a squirrel, a parrot, a cat, an owl, a frog, a snake, a raccoon, a mouse, three dogs, a roadrunner, a goat, a rabbit, a turtle, a spider, and a fish.

Page 20: Buffalo Dancer, #2; Rainbow Dancer, # 4; Harvest Dancer, #1; Butterfly Dancer, #3.

Page 21:

Page 27:

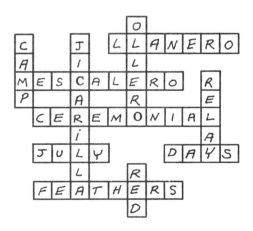

Page 28: Differences are engineer's hat, hair, and pocket; girl's shorts and socks; numbers on engine; line at front of engine; roadrunner's tail.

Page 29: vaqueros, low riders, mariachi, ranchera, salsa, fiestas, tamales, Chimayo, blankets, retablo, bulto, santeros, silver, tin, Cordova, market.

Page 30: The balloons with the four-pointed stars..

Page 31:

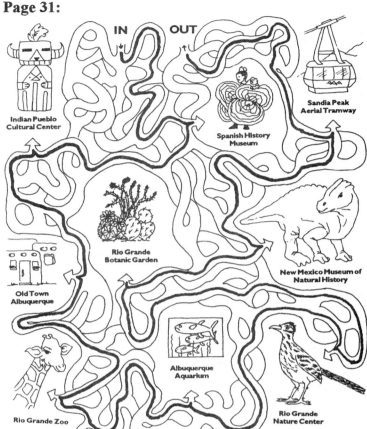

Pages 32-33: Space Hall of Fame, #6; atomic bomb, #4; researchers, #1; Robert Goddard, #3; Very Large Array, #2; Sacramento Peak Observatory, #5.

Page 34:

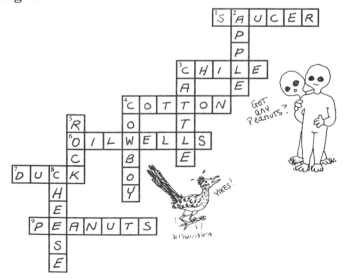

More answers on page 48!

MORE ANSWERS

Page 37:

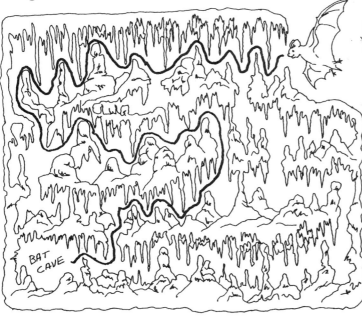

Pages 38-39: pronghorn, jackrabbit, black bear, coyote, prairie dog.

Pages 40-41: Predators are the red-tailed hawk, roadrunner, burrowing owl, and great horned owl.

Page 42:

SCORPIONS are small and very poisonous.

TARANTULAS aren't as bad as they look. They do bite, but they're not poisonous.

GILA MONSTERS are big guys - they grow up to two feet long.

CORAL SNAKES are small but dangerous. Stay away if you see black and red color bands with yellow in between.

DIAMONDBACK RATTLE-SNAKES give a warning shake of their tails when they feel threatened.

A special "muchas gracias" (thank you very much) to:

Sue Sturtevant of the Museum of New Mexico for her helpful suggestions and advice

The Albuquerque Public Library Research Department for their help in verifying facts

The New Mexico Department of Tourism and many city Visitor's Bureaus for providing much helpful information

For more information, call 1-800-545-2040 and ask for a copy of the New Mexico Vacation Guide. It is printed every year and lists the best places to see and things to do all over the Land of Enchantment.